INCIPIENT TETRAD

Viking Zombies

Gripping Horror

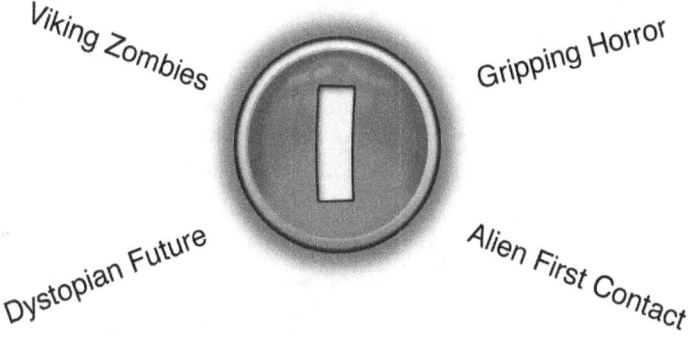

Dystopian Future

Alien First Contact

Futuristic Incarceration

 **4** Short Stories by Best Selling Author:

Hugh B. Long

Published by: Asgard Studios, Ottawa

Visit my website at http://www.hughblong.com

ISBN 978-0-9880896-9-3

About the Author

A little about me (the official bio):

Canadian born Hugh B. Long, who also writes under the pen name Eoghan Odinsson, is an award winning journalist and author.

Graduating from the University of Aberdeen in Scotland with his Masters of Science degree, he subsequently taught for the University, and was a dissertation advisor for graduate students.

In addition to his academic background, Hugh holds a Black Belt in Chito-Ryu Karate, and has taught Martial Arts in Canada and the USA.

He has just returned from a 10-year stretch working in the Washington D.C. area, and is now back in his native Ottawa Valley where he lives with his wife, son and three dogs.

Hugh is a proud Professional Member of the Canadian Authors Association.

Even more about me!

I've been writing for many years, but mostly non-fiction. I've even won two awards, and been nominated for several more! I have to toot my own horn...I'm my own publicist ;)

My interests in fiction are varied: I started off as a young fellow reading Fantasy, such Lord of The Rings and The Hobbit, and absolutely devoured all of Robert E. Howard's Conan Series as a teenager; I later went on to read Science Fiction and Genre Fiction. I have to be honest, I've never been a fan of Literary Fiction.

Some of my favorite authors are: J.R.R. Tolkien, Isaac Asimov, Robert A. Heinlein, David Weber, Jack Campbell (aka John G. Hemry), Ian Douglas, Evan Currie, T.R. Harris, Peter Clines, J.L. Bourne and B.V. Larson.

So what and I working on now, you ask? Well, I'm making the leap from non-fiction into what's termed 'speculative fiction' - essentially Scifi, Fantasy, Horror, Paranormal etc.. that's all considered speculative fiction. Speculative fiction is a sub-genre of the overarching 'Genre Fiction'; I've heard Genre Fiction described as "Ordinary people doing extraordinary things" and Literary fiction described as "Extraordinary people doing ordinary things". I like a good plot, action and interesting characters. I don't disapprove of books focused mostly on character, but I don't want that to be the core of books I read or write - I feel there needs to be a balance. Like a three legged stool: Plot, Action & Character. If any leg of the stool is shorter, the stool falls over - for me anyway.

I'll likely be sticking with Science Fiction and Fantasy, the two genres I most love reading. But don't worry, as Eoghan Odinsson, I'll still be writing non-fiction as well - I take great pride in using the rich and epic mythology of our Northern ancestors, and producing books to highlight interesting aspects of that mythology, spirituality and culture, and you'll likely see that passion seep into my fiction as well! In fact, my first novel is based on Norse Mythology.

As I'm done with all my non-fiction commitments for 2012 (just finished Northern Plant Lore), for at least the next 12 months I'll be focused on my first full length novel: "Dawning of the Wolf Age". It's a tale that blends the best of Norse Mythology with Classic Space Opera. It will be dramatic and wide sweeping (spanning the 100,000 light years of the Milky Way!) My plan is to write a series if it's well received. (Fingers crossed!)

The ETA for the novel to be on the shelves is 2013. I'm not going to promise a date any more specific than that - I'd rather take my time and enjoy the process. If it takes me longer to put out a better book, then that's what I'll do. I won't rush to market to make a bit more money - that's not fun for me, and not fair to you, the reader.

I'll keep interested folks up to date here and on Facebook:

www.facebook.com/TheTribesOfYggdrasil

Of course you can also find me on my website:

www.hughblong.com

Thanks to all my fans!

Table of Contents

Award Winning Author of I'll Buy You The Moon

The Yggdrasíl Codex

A Short Story by: Hugh B. Long

The Yggdrasil Codex

(3200 Words)

In this life there are a great many profound questions that have yet to be answered: Are we the first intelligent life in the universe? Why are we here?

Man continues to ask these questions, apparently to deaf heavens. But what if someone, or something, did answer?

In the short story The Yggdrasil Codex, two University researchers stumble upon an incredible secret encoded on ancient Scandinavian runestones. Their discovery leads them into the world of modern code-breakers and ultimately leads to a revelation with galactic consequences!

Magnus Olsen stood staring intensely at a large slab of grey stone covered with angular inscriptions. He brushed off some dust and continued examining the runic characters, which snaked around the stone inside an anthropomorphic design.

The runes were a very linear looking script that his Viking ancestors used as a system of writing on wood and stone, over a thousand years ago. As a Doctoral candidate in Linguistics at the University of Oslo, Magnus had a passion for the runes that bordered on obsession.

"Oy, Mags!" shouted a young Arab man from the corridor.

"Damn!" Startled, Magnus looked up. "Tariq, why must you do that?" he asked. With a mildly annoyed look, he turned back to the runestone.

"Mags, get your nose off that stone. It's sat a thousand years, bro, surely it can wait. Let's go grab a pint," he said in his Cockney accent.

"Almost ready. Give me five ok?"

Tariq pulled up a stool and sat down beside the runestone, which measured 10 metres long, and was lying on a massive steel frame.

Magnus began scribbling in a tattered notebook, and Tariq started leafing through papers on the table. Tariq replaced the papers and looked over at the section of the runestone Magnus was inspecting.

"Looks like a constellation, mate," Tariq said, leaning closer to Magnus.

"They are runes, my friend, not constellations. I'll make you a bargain: you confine your theories to astrophysics and I will confine mine to linguistics and runology"

"No, seriously, Magnus, look here," Tariq pointed to a series of indented dots between the rows of runes.

"Those dots indicate the end of words," instructed Magnus.

"Yeah, sure, but pretend the runes weren't there - wait a sec, I have an idea." Tariq grabbed a large sheet of blank paper, placed it over the section of runic inscription, and with a pencil, marked only the dots on the paper. Pulling the paper off the stone, he set it on the table and hastily drew lines connecting the points.

"Look! See? It's the constellation Draco," Tariq explained.

Magnus picked up the diagram with a curious look.

Tariq grabbed a second sheet of paper, placed it over a different section of the stone, and shortly produced a second constellation.

Gesturing to the paper, palm down, he said, "Canis Major."

Magnus was stunned. Wide eyed, he slowly lowered himself down onto one of the stools and stared at Tariq.

"Tariq...do you know what this means?"

"Absolutely. It means you're done for the day, and were going to grab a pint ya silly bugger, let's go."

The discovery of constellations, on what was being dubbed the 'Olsen al-Fazari Runestone', sent linguists, historians and astronomers into a frenzy of research and reevaluation of old assumptions. The fact that constellations were encoded onto the stones added an irresistible dimension to this mystery.

Codes on runestone were nothing new, and when deciphered, they almost always yielded simple epitaphs. Occasionally, they would read like magical spells, and given some of these monuments were erected after the conversion to Christianity, the sponsor would certainly want their heretical intentions hidden from plain view, and so, encoded them.

This was the first time in history man discovered inscriptions that went beyond mere commemoration, and further, hinted at the scientific.

Magnus looked out the window of the limousine as they approached the futuristic looking 'Government Communications

Headquarters', or simply 'GCHQ'; affectionately nicknamed the "Doughnut" after its shape. Despite it's humorous moniker, this was the most secure building in all of the United Kingdom. GCHQ was Britain's equivalent to the American's CIA and NSA, and the Doughnut, the Pentagon. In addition to being the home of intelligence gathering, this was the new home of the code-breakers, most famously of Bletchley Park, Britain's code-breaking centre during WWII. This small group became heroes after they cracked the German's "Enigma" cipher machine - considered a key accomplishment in turning the tide of the Second World War.

"Bloody brilliant!" exclaimed Tariq. "I feel like a spook, mate!"

Magnus managed a smile at Tariq, but felt uneasy. He was happiest when poring over old journals, deciphering runic inscriptions, or reading a good book - this cloak and dagger business left him with a pit in his stomach. Why were they here? Surely they could have done more of this decoding back in Oslo? When

Magnus received a telephone call from the Prime Minister asking him to fly to London, he didn't think to raise these objections.

The limousine weaved its way through various security checkpoints, and finally stopped near a large set of doors. Magnus considered the contrast in architecture between the futuristic Doughnut, and the elegant Victorian style of Bletchley Park. 'Progress,' he thought sardonically.

A nondescript man in a grey suit opened the door of the limousine and ushered Magnus and Tariq into the building. After recording their retinal scans, reminding Magnus of his last visit to the ophthalmologist, the visitors were issued badges and directed down a long hall. They progressed through several checkpoints; at each point they pressed an eye to a scanning device and were cleared for entry. The final scanner opened a door into a cavernous room lined with LCD monitors and digital equipment. In the centre of the room stood the Olsen al-Fazari Runestone, around which a dozen or more men and women were buzzing, taking notes and pictures, and chatting in excited tones. The energy in the room was electric, and gradually, the foreboding Magnus felt turned to wonder.

A man with greying hair and dressed in a finely tailored suit walked up and held out a hand to Magnus.

"John Loughheed, Director of GCHQ. Welcome, gentlemen. It's our pleasure to have you here." He shook Tariq's hand in turn. "I'm sorry to have summoned you here so abruptly, but I imagine you will be pleased once we fill you in." The Director nodded his head and gestured to a middle aged man in a white lab coat, who approached the group.

"Allow me to introduce Dr. William Knox from the University of Aberdeen. He's the lead cryptanalyst and head of the project."

"Gentlemen," he said, nodding, and shaking hands with the men.

"Dr. Knox will brief on what we've uncovered over the last few days."

"Aye, well, where to start," Knox pondered. "Well I don't suppose I have to tell you the significance of finding constellations on a runestone; that in itself is a bloody marvel, but there's more to the story lads. We've run the inscriptions on your runestone through our quantum computers - we've got some brilliant equipment here," he smiled, "we discovered that the constellations weren't the only extra bits encoded on the stone. The constellations were more or less in plain sight, but there is some bloody complicated encryption buried in the inscriptions - so complex in fact that there is no way our ancestors did it. They simply didn't have the ability to generate a code of that complexity a thousand years ago, and there's more to the story here than you might have supposed. Don't get me wrong, there were some brilliant men, the equals of any today I'm certain. But the machines we have now to crunch numbers just didn't exist. There wouldn't have been paper enough to compute what we're finding here."

Magnus and Tariq looked at each other, shocked.

"What are you saying, Doc?" asked Tariq

"Och aye, exactly. What am I saying? Well, if I were to apply Occam's razor and choose the simplest explanation with the fewest assumptions, I'd say some clever bastard has pranked us and carved this stone fresh and is sitting back laughing somewhere."

"And is that a possibility?" asked Magnus, "have you carbon dated the stone?"

"Aye, we have."

"And?" urged Tariq.

"It's at least one hundred and eighty thousand years old," he said.

"That's not possible!" Magnus objected, "We were barely walking erect then, and certainly not carving runestones."

"Well, my friends," said Knox, "if I apply Occam's razor yet again, my next guess is that a technologically advanced being carved this stone."

"Are you saying aliens carved this runestone?" asked Magnus.

"Not just this one…" Knox gestured to a second stone standing a few metres away.

Magnus walked over to the second stone and caressed it's surface gently. Tariq followed, shaking his head.

"How many more are there?" Tariq asked.

"We think there are three in all," replied Knox, "so we're looking for one more."

"Why do you assume three?" asked Magnus

"Aye, well I don't need to tell you much about Norse Mythology Magnus, but for Tariq's benefit….the Norse believed there were nine worlds, Earth, or Midgard, being one of them. On the stones we've decoded is a list of some of the names of the nine worlds, and their locations within constellations. On your runestone, for example, you uncovered the constellations Draco, Canis Major and a symbol we believe represents the center of the Milky Way Galaxy. We found the words Muspelheim,

Jotunheim, and Helheim mapped respectively to those symbols. On the second stone, we found the constellations Virgo and Orion. The third symbol seems to be our solar system. Each of these corresponds respectively to Svartalfheim, Niflheim, and Midgard. So we're looking for a third stone which should have the worlds Asgard, Vanaheim and Alfheim listed - that would give us the nine worlds. Haven't a clue what constellations the last three might be mapped to, but we're pretty sure there's a third stone out there, and we think we might be looking in the right area just now!"

The project became known as the "Yggdrasil Codex", in honour of the Norse world tree Yggdrasil that in Norse mythology tied all the nine worlds together.

Magnus and Tariq moved into dormitory housing on the GCHQ campus and spent long days working with Dr. Knox and his team decoding and deciphering the messages on the rune-stones. In a few weeks the third runestone was found which had the constellations Corvus,

Libra and Cygnus; they were indeed mapped to the worlds of Asgard, Vanaheim, and Alfheim.

Dr. Knox was staring intently at his laptop, shaking his head, and called out, "Lads, come over here for a minute."

Magnus and Tariq, who were sitting at desks a few metres away in the open plan room, got up and walked over to Dr. Knox.

"S'up Docta Knox?" said Tariq.

"Look at this." He pointed to the screen. The word 'hættr' was displayed on the screen. "What do you make of that Magnus?"

"It just means *dangerous*... in Old Norse," he replied.

"Och aye, thats what I thought." Knox's fingers clattered over the keyboard and a new string of text appeared on the screen. He looked back over his shoulder at Magnus.

Magnus bent over looking closer. "*Travel not to these dangerous lands*," he translated, "What is that in reference to?"

"That was also encrypted on your runestone. I think it's a warning of sorts," replied Knox.

Magnus looked puzzled, "A warning from what? These are constellations."

"No bro, I think they're being more specific," said Tariq, "remember, each of these constellations is tied to one of the nine worlds. In Libra, we have Vanaheim, and remember we discovered Kepler 22b there a couple of years back. That's a real planet bro. I would guess there must be planets corresponding to each of these other worlds. We just haven't got any proof they exist yet, except for Kepler 22b."

"Ok," Magnus nodded.

"Now here's a real mind blower, gentlemen," Tariq continued, "V4641 Sgr., in the Sagitarius constellation, isn't a planet…"

"What is it?" asked Knox.

"It's a bloody Black Hole!"

Several months passed, and anyone else working sixteen hours days might have been at their wits end, but with the magnitude of their discoveries, the team was as energized as the day they started - there was no greater mystery being researched in history.

Thousands of additional hours of quantum-computer processing revealed the locations of objects, presumably planets, surrounding specific stars in each of the constellations. The team now had precise coordinates where they could aim the Hubble space telescope and some of the earth-bound radio telescopes, such as the massive dish at Arecibo. While they did this, the GCHQ quantum-computer continued to relentlessly analyze additional detail on the rune-stones.

Tariq was standing in front of a computer screen that filled an entire wall; on it glowed a map of the constellations and objects they were studying. Data flashed on the screen, including distance between objects, spectral classes of the stars and other astronomical minutiae. Magnus walked up, touching his shoulder.

"How's it going?"

"Incredible…" Tariq whispered, not taking his eyes of the screen.

"What is? You need to be more specific, I'm a linguist, not an Astronomer," he joked.

"Well, bro, neither am I. I'm an Astrophysicist, not an Astronomer. If you'd quit playing with your stones you might learn a few things." He laughed at Magnus.

"Ok, game face," Tariq said, "what I'm staring at is the distances between the planets. If this stone was carved by aliens, where are they now? Space is vast, brother, how the bloody hell did they get here and back again? It's not like a trip to Mars that might take us a couple of years; we're talking millions of times farther. So how did they do it?"

Magnus look puzzled. "Good question."

"I think we need to be looking for clues on the runestones. If these wee spacemen put the damn things here and gave us warnings, surely we were meant to communicate with them?"

wondered Tariq, "I'm going to ask Knox to add several additional parameters to the quantum-computer analysis. There has to be more here that we aren't seeing."

Several days later Magnus and Tariq were at breakfast in the cafeteria, where Tariq was flirting shamelessly with a young intern from Dublin.

"You Irish girls have the most beautiful accent," he said, "you know, I think I'm part Irish, on my mother's side."

Magnus lowered his head in embarrassment as he listened to Tariq's cheesy pick up lines. Although he thought Tariq was shameless, he secretly wished for that confidence to talk to women - ironic since he was a linguist.

Dr. Knox burst into the cafeteria. "Lads! Come quick!" He turned around and dashed out again.

Magnus and Tariq looked at each other puzzled. Magnus got up with his cafeteria tray and walked off to follow Knox. Tariq leaned over, gently picked up the young woman's hand, kissed it, winked, and ran off to join Magnus.

As they entered the lab, the entire team was gathered around one of the large wall monitors where line after line of equations were scrolling down. The scientists whispering to each other, shaking their heads, looking on with awe and reverence.

"What is it?" Magnus asked.

"Instructions!" Knox replied, shaking with excitement.

"What sort of instructions?" Tariq inquired.

"Tariq, you know what tachyons are of course?" Knox inquired.

"Of course."

"Hey, so do I!" said Magnus laughing, "I watch Star Trek! They're particles that move faster than light. But the experiment with the neutrinos back in 2010 that declared their existence was found to be in error, right?"

"It was, but these instructions demonstrate how to work around that!" Knox's voice was almost shrill with excitement.

"So what now?" Magnus asked.

"We build it. The instructions show how to take advantage of what we call an Einstein-Rosen bridge - a wormhole. The device will create a microscopic wormhole between our location in space-time and the destination, and through that wormhole we can send a data transmission."

It was another few months before the team, now tripled in size since the project's inception, was able to build the Einstein-Rosen Bridge Transceiver (ERBT). It was a modestly sized device, tubular, a metre in diameter, and maybe three meters long. It looked like a fat telescope mounted on a tripod and hooked up to some thick cables. The transceiver was connected to a video camera and to the large wall display unit, so for all intents and purposes the system was really just an advanced video conferencing system.

The device had been tested in loopback mode, so they knew that all inputs and outputs worked, the unknown was whether the tachyon transceiver would function as predicted. There was nothing left but a live test.

The team gathered in the lab, standing silently, each of them barely breathing. As head of the project team, Dr. Knox had the honour of 'throwing the switch' and initiating the call. The deciphered instructions had them point the transceiver in the direction of Kepler 22b, the newly recently planet in the Cygnus constellation.

With trembling hands he pressed a key on a laptop that initiated the call, and held his breath.

The machine sprang to life with a deep whine resonating inside the room - everyone felt it's power in their bodies, like being at a concert. The whine morphed into a steady thrumming, and people began to breath again.

The video screen on the wall flickered, and lit up with a white light. Slowly the white darkened and a slender female figure began to appear. She had blonde hair, and had a very human appearance, but slightly more delicate and fine featured - not very alien at all.

"I am Aeronwen," she said with a lyrical voice, "we expected you would contact us one day. We greet you now warmly, as brothers and sisters," she opened her arms in a welcoming gesture.

The team was stunned, shocked, horrified, and elated in equal measure.

"I...I'm Dr. Knox, head of the project team," he said.

"We are happy to meet you Dr. Knox," she replied, lowering her head respectfully.

"I don't know where to start..." Knox trailed off.

"Who are you?" Tariq asked.

"We are the Alfar."

"Did you create us?" asked Magnus.

"Oh, no, not us." Aeronwen smiled. "Your progenitors are the Aesir. They did not create you exactly, they simply added what you might call a divine spark, shaping what you would become. We Alfar are just your brothers and sisters of sorts. We were asked to shepherd your race when your time came to start traveling among the nine worlds. The runestones were placed by the Aesir as a test. Once you advanced enough to decipher their hidden secrets, that knowledge enabled you to contact us and we would know you were ready for our guidance."

"So the Aesir gave birth to the Alfar as well?" Tariq asked.

"No, our progenitors were the Vanir. They are the second of the three elder races, the others being the Jotuns."

"I have so many questions," Knox said.

"But why?" asked Magnus.

"Why?" repeated Aeronwen, looking puzzled.

"Why did the Aesir get involved with us? What do they want from us?" Magnus asked.

Aeronwen smiled, "Do you have a flower garden?"

"Yes, my mother does."

"Why does she garden?" Aeronwen asked?

Magnus just stared at her, not quite sure how to answer that question.

"The gods and goddesses tend to us like we were a flower garden," Aeronwen continued, "they marvel at our beauty and diversity, they take pride in helping us grow, they seed us through the stars. They are like our gardeners."

THE END

From the Award Winning Author of "The Yggdrasil Codex"

Draugr's Saga: Part 1

Real Zombie Vikings!

LET SLEEPING DRAUGS LIE

A short story by: Hugh B. Long

Let Sleeping Draugs Lie

(6409 words)

It's Erik Ragnarsson's first summer raiding season. With his new ship Ottar, and his very own crew, Erik sets out for glory and wealth.

A freak storm blows them off course and when they make landfall, things are not as they seem.

Erik and his foster brother, Arndt, must work together to battle fellow crew, and a great evil stalking the island!

A cool evening breeze chilled the old man's bones. He shivered and pulled his cloak tight about him, moving forward to stoke the fire. Although it was summer, this far north when the gift of the sun's warmth waned, a chill stole back into the world.

Three children ran up to the fire, chasing each other in some sort of game, a very noisy game; the old man didn't like noisy games.

"You there! Be still lest you draw the evil spirit to our camp," the old man said.

The three children stopped and looked at him with looks of horror mixed with curiosity in equal measure.

"Evil spirits? They don't exist. My father says that's nonsense," said the biggest child, a boy with red hair.

"They don't?" Asked the old man. "Really? Well, that's a relief! Then I must have dreamed this - "

The old man pulled up his sleeve revealing a stump. The children were startled and pulled back. The little girl seemed a bit braver than the two boys and moved forward for a closer look.

"An evil spirit took your hand?" She asked, reaching out with a finger to touch the metal cap over the old mans stump.

"You are a brave young woman. But no, in fact an evil spirit did not take my hand, but I have fought them before." The old man pulled up his sleeve to cover the stump, then pulled it back down again revealing a hand. The children gasped in amazement.

The two boys moved back towards the old man. The second boy, the youngest of the three, said, "Will you tell us the tale? Please?"

The old man wrinkled his brow and frowned, looking from child to child. "Well...I suppose these are things you are old enough to learn. Are you all brave enough to hear it?"

They nodded enthusiastically.

"Alright then. Fetch a couple of logs then come and sit by the fire."

The frigid waves smashed the longship, leaping over the sides of the boat and soaking the men inside. They had long since reefed the sail and now were focused on steering her into the waves to stay afloat. Some of the younger crew asked why they didn't bring the boat to shore; the older, more seasoned men explained that it was much riskier to try to get to shore in a storm. In strange lands no man knew where a deadly reef or other hazard might lurk beneath the surface, waiting to bring the men to their deaths.

For hours the pilot did battle with the tiller. It kicked and jarred him, and on several occasions would have thrown him overboard had he not been lashed to it. Many men were sick, offering up to the sea what little they had in their stomachs. The sky was lit with lightning and they could hear Thor doing battle with giants, for his hammer made a great thunderous noise that followed the flashes.

Almost three days passed and the storm finally abated; the crew were spent. Their wool tunics were all soaked with sea water, but thankfully,

29

even when wet, the wool provided great warmth.

Although the rain relented, a dark blanket of cloud still hung over them menacingly, blocking their view of the sun, by which they navigated during the day.

Erik Ragnarsson was a big man, even by the standards of his people. This was his first summer raid with his own ship. He had accompanied his father on raids for five summers and acquitted himself bravely. He had earned enough silver over those seasons to buy his own boat. It wasn't a new boat, but the Ottar was Erik's; this was his crew, his raid.

Erik stood at the stern of the boat, gazing out over the vast sea, his hand shielding his eyes.

"What do you see, Lord?" asked Sven Gardarsson, a grizzled veteran.

"Little of nothing, Sven. Aegir has seen fit to blow us well off course." Erik pulled a yellowish crystal from a pouch on his belt and held it up to his eye. As he held the sunstone up, he turned his body until it lit up, indicating the direction of the sun; now they at least knew their direction of travel. "Keep us on a westerly course, Sven. I believe we should still be close to the Land of Eir. My cousin Thorfinn is awaiting our arrival to begin the siege. I do not want to disappoint him."

"Aye, Lord." Sven put his shoulder into the tiller and the Ottar's planks groaned as she flexed and rippled under pressure from the pounding waves, slowly turning onto a Westerly course.

Erik could hear his men laughing, which was usually a good sign. After three days battling the storm they were thirsty, hungry and tired. He saw a fire in the brazier. Good, he thought. Some hot soup would be nice.

Ivarr Haraldsson was laughing at one of the younger crewman, Arndt. "You sad little bastard! Look! He pissed himself," Ivarr said, pointing to the young man's stained crotch. Arndt had been a thrall, but was now a free man, a Karl. Erik's father captured Arndt during a raid on Eir, ten years past, and had freed the boy just this Spring. He was like a little brother to Erik, but as a former Thrall, was not well regarded by the other Karls. It was not unprecedented for former Thralls to do very well after being freed. In the North, actions spoke louder than accidents of birth.

Ivarr was laughing and encouraging the other men to join his mockery. Erik strode down to the middle deck near the fire and stood beside Ivarr, a foot taller and significantly thicker.

"What revelry have I missed?" He asked with a curious smile.

"We were just noticing evidence of Arndt's courage," the man smiled, "see, he pissed himself," Ivarr pointed to the boy's pants, looking around for support.

"I see." Erik nodded "Is that a trick you taught him, Ivarr? I seem to remember you pissing yourself a couple of summers ago in the shield wall." Erik said evenly, raising an eyebrow.

Ivarr's face went red with fury. Erik could see the man's hand on the handle of his seax (a short belt knife).

"I had to piss before that battle," he seethed, "I drank much ale with the men to celebrate our upcoming victory."

"Ah, yes, I hear ale does help build courage. Did it work?" Erik asked.

Ivarr drew his seax in a flash, but just as fast, a man behind him grabbed his sword arm and a second grabbed his shield arm, dragging him back. Ivarr was frothing at the mouth.

Erik appeared to be completely unfazed by this attempted assault. "Excellent, Ivarr! Lets hope you can muster that same fury in the face of the Celts." Erik stepped forward and whispered in Ivarr's ear as the others held him, "If you ever draw a blade on me again, you piece of weasel piss, I'll cut off your balls and feed them to you." He patted Ivarr on the shoulder and smiled.

Ivarr's face relaxed. He realized he had just been saved. Had his blade reached Erik, he would have been lucky to survive the encounter, unless he struck a lucky blow; Erik was a formidable warrior. Had he miraculously killed Erik, his banner men would have been honor bound to kill Ivarr; either way he would have been dead.

Ivarr shook off his saviors and walked to the bow of the ship.

Arndt offered Erik a cup of soup. "Thank you, Arndt," Erik said.

As the youngest crewman, Arndt was relegated to performing some of the more menial tasks during the voyage. But as a Thrall he had ten years of experience and took them on willingly; anything to allow him the opportunity for him to earn some silver on this voyage. He was conflicted at first; this raid was on his own countrymen, but he was so young when he was taken from them, that he felt more at home in the fjords than in the hills of Eir.

Erik sipped the steaming soup gingerly. "How is it?" Arndt asked.

"Tastes like hot piss. But it's warm." He winked at Arndt. Erik loved his foster brother. Arndt was a few years younger, but the boys had spent ten years together growing up on the same farmstead. Erik's father always treated Arndt well; all the Thralls on Ragnar's farmstead were treated with dignity. He brooked no disrespect or disobedience though, and if they worked hard, they were treated like family and eventually freed.

"Erik!" A young man named Einar yelled out. "Land!"

Erik made his way back to the stern and the tiller platform which was raised above the rowing benches. He could indeed see land. He just hoped it was Eir.

As the Ottar slid towards the unknown shore, several men jumped into the sea and pulled her up onto the strand, beaching her. Erik, now in his mail armor, with his sword and shield, jumped off the prow and onto the rocky sand. He stood and surveyed the area in front the ship. Sven walked up and stood beside him.

"So, my Lord, is this Eir?" Asked Sven.

"Look around, Sven. Tell me what you see."

Sven looked confused, but attempted an answer. "Grass and sand, my Lord?"

"There are no trees. Not a single tree." Erik looked over at Sven. "What do you make of that?"

"Perhaps the Celts cut them down?"

"All of them?" Erik asked. "Then where are the stumps?"

Erik and Sven walked the beach for an hour in each direction, and saw not a single tree or shrub. There were grassy mounds everywhere, as far as they could see inland. It was like a rolling sea of mounds and hills. It was the strangest land Erik had ever seen; each mound was tall enough so that you couldn't see from valley to valley.

Back at the Ottar, Erik ordered the men to make camp for the night. They pitched tents and started a proper fire that warmed them all. Thankfully there was a great supply of driftwood, the lack of trees would have made a fire impossible otherwise.

Erik and Arnd pitched their tent; there were six more tents, with four men to a tent, arranged in a semi-circle around the fire.

Tonight would mark the first hot meal in several days - not counting Arndt's soup. To improve spirits, Erik broke out a small barrel of his own mead for the men.

Around the fire men told their tales of shield wall bravado, maidens conquered and treasure found. Erik remembered some of the tales from previous summers and they seem to grow more impossible with each telling.

Arndt came and sat beside Erik.

"What do you intend for tomorrow, Erik?" Arndt asked.

"I think we'll sail north up the coast until we see something familiar."

Arndt sipped some mead.

"Listen," Erik said in a low voice, "the next time that bastard insults you, challenge him. Do not allow your honor to be shit on. You are part of Ragnar's household, Arndt. Even though you are not his son by blood, your acts are tied to our family. Do you understand?"

Arndt nodded.

"I love as if you were my brother by blood, Arndt. I will back you in any fight. You are no longer a Thrall, you are a Karl of Ragnar Eriksson - act like it!"

Ten years of being subservient had left Arndt meek. He was not used to having the option of speaking back when insulted, and although Erik had trained with him recently, he was very new to handling a sword. Erik had been taught to hold a blade from the time he could walk.

"I'll try, Erik. I promise."

Every night when the men were away for home and raiding, they posted a watch. There was always a chance the raiders would be attacked, or worse, their ship. If their ship was destroyed they might be stranded in a foreign land.

During the first watch, just an hour after the first men lay down to get some sleep, the guards heard screaming. In fact the screaming was loud enough to wake everyone.

Erik threw off his blanket and scrambled out of his tent, sword in hand.

"What the fuck is going on?" Erik demanded.

"I'm not sure my Lord. We heard screaming from over near that mound," the guard said, pointing.

Several other men scrambled out of their tents. Erik pointed to one of them. "You! Get four more men to come with me." The man scrambled back into his tent to grab his sword, then dashed off to gather some men.

Erik, and four of his men, accompanied by Arndt, walked cautiously towards the source of the screaming. Each had their weapon ready, whether a sword, a spear or axe. They scrambled up and down two mounds until they saw a torch laying on the ground and a man beside it - Ivarr.

"What in Niflheim are you doing?" Erik barked. Ivarr was sitting, panting, gasping for breath and holding his wrist.

"It atta - attacked us." He stammered

"Who attacked you?" Erik asked. The other men were looking around, now on high alert. It wasn't unheard of for villagers to kill a straggler from camp. Some got brave while the bulk of the Northmen were sleeping.

"It came out of the mound. I tried to fight it off, but it got Gjurd!" Ivarr was trembling.

"Where is Gjurd?" Erik asked

"At the mound"

"We're surrounded by fucking mounds, you idiot! Which mound? Where? Point or something," Erik turned to Arndt, "help him up." Erik had a disgusted look on his face.

Arndt reluctantly helped his antagonist to his feet. When Ivarr saw it was Arndt, he pushed him away.

Erik glared at Ivarr. "Lead us to him."

Ivarr, still trembling, and glancing back to ensure he wasn't alone, walked hesitantly up the hill and west.

Six mounds over, they found Gjurd in front of a hole in the mound. He was bloodied and still. As they got closer they noticed a large wound on his neck; also, there was a freshly dug pile of dirt in front of the hole.

"Did you two imbeciles dig this hole?" Erik asked.

"We were just exploring and we saw a ring on the ground. We figured that these might be burial mounds, so we dug a little and found more treasure - he held up a few silver coins. We kept on digging and found a door to the mound. We thought there would be more gold and silver in there," Ivarr grimaced, "but...we found something else. There was a corpse in the mound."

"What did you expect if you thought it was a grave mound?" Erik shook his head.

One of his men was examining Gjurd.

"Is he dead?" Erik asked.

"Aye, Lord, he's good and dead. There's a chunk bit clean out of his neck. Looks like teeth marks."

Erik glared at Ivarr. Was this man a cannibal? He had heard stories...

Gjurd twitched, and the man examining him jumped back, startled.

"Good and dead you say?" Erik asked. "Take Gjurd back to camp and tend to his wound." And take Ivarr back as well, looks like he injured his wrist," Erik stormed back off to camp.

Arndt was curious. If it was a grave mound, there could be fabulous treasure in there. Great lords were buried with their best weapons, gold, and even slaves and animals. Surely a peek wouldn't hurt, Arndt thought.

He crept up to the freshly dug hole, his torch thrust well ahead of him to light the way. He struggled through the small hole and peered into the mound. He was hoping he would be able to see enough from the entrance to judge whether a deeper trek was in order, but there was a bend in the tunnel preventing a straight view in.

He continued crawling on all fours. As he made his way in he stopped dead and gasped. There was a corpse facing him. It had a seax through its head. It looked like someone thrust up through its chin; the tip of the seax was protruding from the top of its skull. The corpse was shriveled and desiccated; it was most certainly dead. The other two probably just panicked. But how did Gjurd get the bite on his neck? Surely Ivarr didn't do that?

Arndt pushed past the corpse and into the burial chamber. He was disappointed to find it empty. There were no mounds of silver and gold, no chests of jewels. The few coins Ivarr found, must have been the whole treasure.

There were piles of cloth wrappings that were mouldy and stank so much that Arndt had to suppress retching at the scent.

He was about to exit when he saw a bundle in the far corner of the mound. It was wrapped in something different from the burial shroud. He scrambled over to it and prodded it carefully. It looked like an oiled leather bundle. Arndt delicately unwrapped the bundle and inside discovered a long-seax. It was fashioned with a single sided blade like the shorter seax, but was nearly the length of a sword. Many men preferred a long-seax in the shield wall, and stabbed enemies with it in the fashion of the Romans.

It was beautiful. The blade had wavy patterns that seemed to dance under the torch light, and the handle was carved ivory. The blade had several runes on it, but Arndt could not read them. He would have to ask Erik. His face beamed with delight, and he quickly wrapped the long-seax back up in its protective leather package for the journey back to camp.

Back at camp, Arndt saw Erik sitting by the fire. He looked to be in a foul mood. Erik liked his sleep, and was especially grumpy when disturbed. Beside the fire, a young man was tending to Gjurd's wound. Gjurd lay there moaning and fidgeting and Arndt walked over to check on the man.

"Gods he reeks!" said Arndt.

"You all smell like goat shit after four days at sea," Erik said.

"No, Erik, he smells like death." Arndt nearly choked, and stepped away from Gjurd, back towards Erik.

Gjurd continued moaning and seemed to be getting agitated.

"Erik," Arndt said in a whisper, "I found something." Arndt unwrapped the tip of the long-seax and showed Erik while glancing around to make sure nobody saw it.

"It has runes on it, but I cannot read them."

Erik motioned to Arndt and turned his back away from the fire, and the other men. "Show me."

Arndt carefully unwrapped his prize and presented it hilt first to Erik for inspection.

Erik examined the length of the weapon. "That is a beautiful blade, Arndt."

"But what does it say?" Arndt asked, getting impatient.

"Just hold your tongue you little goat turd, I'll get to it."

Erik read each rune in turn, starting from the hilt and working towards the tip of the blade. "D, R, A, U, G, S, B, A, N, E." Erik had a look of shock on his face. "Arndt, this might be a very special weapon; it could have been made by the dark elves in their underworld forges. The inscription reads 'Draug's bane'. You remember father's stories about the Draugr?"

Arndt nodded. He remembered very well. Ragnar used to regale the children with stories of evil spirits who rose up from the dead to torment men - The Draugr. Arndt thought they were only stories.

"This, my brother, is a weapon fit for a Jarl," Erik said.

Arndt had a moment of panic. Did Erik intend to keep it for himself?

"I hope you fight well with it, little brother," Erik said with a smile, and handed the weapon back to Arndt.

Arndt beamed.

Behind them Gjurd began to wail very loudly and thrash wildly. Erik and Arndt turned back to him.

"Poor bastard...He's probably been poisoned by Ivarr's bite. I've seen men die from a bite suffered in battle. I knew of a man who's ear was bitten off my a Celt. He died a week later," Erik said.

As a Arndt watched, he felt his hands grow warm. He looked down and there was a bluish glow surrounding the blade of his long-seax. "What in Niflheim?"

The man tending Gjurd screamed and they saw him biting the man. He jumped up and away from Gjurd. "You bastard! I was trying to help you!" shouted the young man.

Gjurd got to his feet and shambled after the young man. His eyes, Arndt noticed - they were milky white orbs.

Erik ran up to Gjurd and grabbed him by the shoulder and spun him around. As he did so, Gjurd bit Erik's wrist. Erik responded to the bite with a punch that would have leveled an ox. Gjurd fell down, but began scrambling back up. Several other men came over and jumped on Gjurd, wrestling with him. They were soon yelling that they too had been bitten.

"It seemed Gjurd has a taste for men's flesh." Sven said. "My Lord, I think he's gone mad. It would be a kindness if we put him down."

"Aye," Erik said. He thought for a moment then unsheathed his sword. "Hold him down," he ordered.

Four men held Gjurd's limbs and Erik thrust his sword deep into the man's belly, clear through into the sand beneath him. But Gjurd continued to writhe and moan.

"What the fuck?" Erik said in confusion.

Erik thrust thrice more, and Gjurd still continued to groan and thrash.

The men holding Gjurd leapt up and scrambled back, terrified at the 'thing' in front of them. Gjurd ambled towards the group of men, and several with spears held him at bay; their spears actually piercing Gjurd's torso, but Gjurd kept pushing against him.

"Gods! That's unnatural," Sven said.

"Burn him!" One of the men shouted.

"You! Grab a torch!" Erik shouted.

A torch was tossed to Erik who caught it and immediately thrust it at the back of Gjurd, who was focused on another man currently holding him at bay with a spear. Gjurd's clothing burst into flame, but he appeared not to notice it at all.

One of the larger veterans, touting a two handed Danish axe, walked up to Gjurd and cleaved through his shoulder, splitting him like a chicken. Gjurd still refused to die! He was a smoking, shambling, half-split man, one arm and shoulder drooping right to the ground.

Several other men ran up, taking turns attacking Gjurd with seax, sword, spear and axe. None stopped him, but several were bitten and scratched in the process.

Arndt was afraid. He let the other more experienced men make the initial attacks, but as they seemed to be wholly ineffective, he decided to act. He forced courage to the front of his mind and ran at Gjurd screaming a high pitched battle cry; it sounded more like a young girl getting her hair pulled. He slashed at Gjurd with his long-seax, the blue blade glowing brightly. Gjurd began to scream and howl - in pain! Arndt was hurting him, and Gjurd was on the retreat; but he was still standing.

Gjurd now resembled a tenderized roast that had also been sliced, with bits of his meat falling onto the strand as he moved around.

Arndt grabbed the long-seax with both hands and aimed a powerful blow at Gjurd's head, which came off as easily as knocking a jug off a wall. The blade's blue glow diminished and Gjurd ceased thrashing.

Exhausted, Arndt dropped to the ground and let his weapon sink into the sand. The men cheered and gave thanks to Arndt Draug Slayer.

"Well done, brother!" Erik patted him on the shoulder and helped him up. Arndt grabbed at his weapon, retrieving his long-seax. "Come, you have well and truly earned some mead!"

It was the middle of the night, but none of the men were going to get any rest this night, they were just too excited from their brush with the evil Draug. Several of the men burned the rest of Gjurd's body, just to be sure.

Fully half of Erik's crew had been wounded fighting Gjurd. Ivarr had bandaged up his wrist, but was looking very ill, and lay curled up in front of the fire.

"I never imagined your father's tales were true, Erik." Arndt said.

"Nor I. We shall never doubt him again, eh?"

Arndt nodded.

"You were brave tonight," Erik said, "I was proud to call you my banner man. So proud in fact, that I think we have some business."

Arndt looked puzzled. Erik stood up.

"Men! Hear me! Tonight, I have a new brother. I, Erik Ragnarsson, take Arndt as my blood brother!" He motioned for Arndt to stand.

Arndt stood, mouth agape. Erik took Draug's Bane from Arndt's hand and drew its blade sharply across his palm. Blood flowed freely from the long incision. He handed it back to Arndt, who assumed he was to do the same. He repeated the cut to his hand. Erik then clasped his bloody palm to Arndt's, sealing the pact.

"Henceforth you shall be know as Arndt Ragnarsson. If any man disputes this, let him stand before me now." Erik glared into the crowd. The men seemed genuinely pleased for

Arndt's elevation and none came forward to challenge the adoption. Arndt had slain a Draug tonight - few men could make that claim. And even though he was a young warrior with no experience in the shield wall, he threw himself into danger when he saw it was needed. That was all his company needed to know. In the shield wall, the man beside you could save your life or spell your doom. Arndt proved to be the former.

Erik hugged him tightly, then grabbed at his stomach in sudden pain.

"Erik, are you alright?" Arndt asked.

"Yes, yes, I'm fine. Must have been that piss you fed me on the boat." Erik smiled weekly. "I think I just need some rest."

Several of the men seemed to be suffering from stomach ailments, and were variously groaning, writhing or clasping at their guts.

Erik went to his tent to lay down.

What had previously been a celebration now felt like the morning after. Arndt sat quietly beside the fire and polished Draug's Bane, cleaning off the blood and gore. He saw Ivarr on the other side of the fire, glaring back at him. He could feel the man's venomous stare as if they were a serpent's teeth sinking into his skin. Ivarr was trouble, and Arndt knew their dealings were not yet concluded.

Arndt was curled up sitting in front of the fire, just at the edge of sleep, his head nodding down. Then Arndt heard a shuffling, and saw Ivarr stand up. Draug's Bane was glowing blue in his lap, and Arndt leapt to his feet. He could see Ivarr's eyes - dead milky white orbs, boring into his brain, and…Ivarr was smiling!

"Erik!" Arndt shouted, while holding Draug's Bane in front of him, pointed at his foe. Ivarr seemed to pull back when he saw the blade.

"That's right, you stinking piece of shit. I am Arndt, Draug Slayer!" He paused as he saw Ivarr's head twist and his shoulders flex. Was he getting bigger? Gods! Ivarr was growing taller! And wider!

Erik stumbled out of the tent looking pale. Several other men were up now, all looking seasick or hungover, through they were on dry land and had little to drink.

Ivarr laughed at Arndt. Ivarr now stood at least a head above Erik, and was much wider. Erik looked shocked. Ivarr had been a much smaller man that Erik just an hour ago.

"Men," shouted Erik weakly, "get to the boat! This place is cursed. I will hold Ivarr. Go! You too, Arndt!"

"No, I will not leave my brother!" Arndt said.

Erik thrust his sword deep into Ivarr's back while he was focused on Arndt. Ivarr reacted like a fly had landed on him, and back handed Erik, sending him flying into his tent and collapsing it.

Ivarr pointed a rotting finger at Arndt. His flesh was decayed, as if he was a corpse. And the stench! It was worse than poor Gjurd.

Arndt slashed his long-seax at Ivarr, who just smiled, and seemed to grow yet bigger. Arndt leaped towards Ivarr and cut across his left wrist, severing it completely. Ivarr howled, but did not retreat. Why was nobody helping him? There were over twenty men in camp and not one came to his aid. Useless bastards, Arndt thought.

Arndt heard a noise behind him and saw one of the other crewmen, but he was not coming to help - his eyes were also milky white, and he stank. He was coming for Arndt as well!

"Erik! Help me!" Arndt screamed.

Erik heard his brother's cry and got up from the wreckage of his tent, and stumbled over to help his brother. Arndt was trying to keep both of these Draugr in front him now. Knew he had to act decisively. He couldn't hope to fight two of them - he needed to kill one of them very quickly. He saw an opening and lunged forward, and with both hands, decapitated the other Draugr. The headless corpse dropped to the ground like a sack of flour, and made no further sound.

That left Ivarr. Erik grabbed Ivarr from behind in a bear hug, but Erik's arms would barely surround Ivarr now. Ivarr threw his head backward and Arndt heard a sickening crunch; Erik fell back to the ground, his face a bloody mess.

"Arndt, get to the boat!" Erik yelled. He grabbed onto Ivar's ankles and held tight. "Go! Go!"

Arndt ran to the boat and saw men trying to push her out into the waves; they were struggling. Arndt joined in and his extra weight helped the Ottar slide off the strand and into the water. He clambered aboard.

He looked back and saw that Erik had put his seax through Ivarr's foot and had him pinned to the ground.

"Erik! Leave him, run to the boat!" Arndt shouted, but it was no use. He saw Ivarr bend over and bite Erik, coming back up with a full mouth of flesh. Erik stopped moving.

"No!" screamed Arndt. A tear ran down his cheek as he watched his brother's still body.

Ivarr managed to get the Seax out of his foot and was running towards the boat. Nine other former crewmen joined him, also now Draugr. The group groaned and reached for the boat, but seemed unable to enter the water. Thank the gods, Arndt thought. He slumped down and cried as the remaining crew rowed the Ottar away from shore.

Hours later Arndt awoke, hoping he had been having a nightmare, but no, Erik was nowhere to be seen.

The crew that remained, all looked very ill; he saw them lying in between the benches clutching their stomachs. He also saw that Draug's Bane was glowing - ever so slightly. His blood went icy cold, and he listened. He pulled out his Mjollnir amulet from beneath his tunic and held it between his thumb and forefinger, and prayed to Thor. His people had prayed to different gods; he thought he remembered one named Lugh, but no matter, Thor was his god now. He hoped Thor would come and smite these evil creatures.

His mind raced and he thought about what might happen if these beasts made it back to the fjords. Gods! They would all become Draugr! Arndt had to do something, but he didn't want to sacrifice himself. He was a young man, and had only started venturing out in the world. Surely the gods would not be that cruel?

He couldn't kill them all, especially in these confined quarters. He could burn them, but then the boat would burn too and that would leave him swimming at sea. The fire seemed to have no effect on them anyway. They didn't like the sea, he thought. Was there anyway he could get them in the water?; Not all of them.

That was the only real solution to his problem - he had to burn the boat. Arndt crept over to the mast and the brazier. He watched the men around him as he lit a fire and put on a pot, ostensibly to boil water. He also took some straw used for bedding, and some fat for cooking and dropped bits of it around the boat as he walked amongst the men. Draug's Bane was glowing more brightly now and he could see the men looking sicker, and the stench!

With all of them sick, Arndt had taken to stuffing bits of oily cloth up his nose to dampen the smell.

Once he was ready, he kicked over the brazier and the hot coals spread all around the deck. The bits of straw and fat caught fire immediately, and Arndt was shocked at how fast the blaze spread. Men began moaning but they were still all too sick to get up and deal with the fire.

Arndt ran to the stern of the boat where the tiller was. The tiller (the portion on deck) and the rudder (the portion in the water) was massive piece of wood. It might be enough to allow Arndt to float like a small raft. He just had to get it loose from the ship. There were several wooden pegs holding it together, and he started trying to knock them loose and free the rudder. The first came out with little trouble but the second one took him longer, all the while the fire spread rapidly aft and stern. Two more to go.

Several of the men were standing now, confused and shambling around the boat.

Arndt was desperately working on the third peg. Done. The fourth and final peg, and the tightest. He heard one of the Draugr coming up towards him. Arndt stood and swung at the thing's head, which was in a perfect position to be decapitated. Off went the head, and Arndt went back the fourth peg.

He bashed at it with the hilt of Draug's Bane and saw part of it come free. More moans and shuffling feet approached the stern. He struggled with the last peg, the flames now licking dangerously close to him. Most of the Draugr were on fire, but still moving around. The ship was ablaze and Arndt could feel his cheeks burning under the radiant heat. Another Draugr stuck its head up and climbed the steps to the tiller platform. Arndt focused on the last peg...he had to get that out before the ship went down, otherwise, he would be burnt alive.

The Draug sank its teeth deep into Arndt's shoulder and he screamed, dropping his weapon. He tripped and fell on his back with the Draug clambering for him. Arndt lunged for his long-seax, grabbed it, and jumped to his

61

feet. The Draug was near the edge of the ship and Arndt ran forward with a kick, sending the Draug over the ship and plummeting into the sea. It sank swiftly beneath the waves.

Arndt pushed back on the tiller peg. The fire was now an inferno; his cheeks were blistered from the heat. The last peg came loose and Arndt kicked it free. With a great splash, the rudder and tiller fell beneath the ship. Arndt dove off the back of the ship and plunged into the freezing North Sea.

As he swam to up from the depths, he could see the red blaze above him on the surface. Flickering and dancing - it was beautiful he thought, almost serene. He broke the water and gasped. He hadn't needed air so much, but after the heat of the fire the sea was like ice.

He tread water and looked for the rudder. He saw it! It was bobbing several ship-lengths astern of the Ottar. He swam desperately to his last chance for life. As he reached the rudder, he climbed aboard and collapsed. He had enough strength to roll over and face the burning ship. The Northmen dreamt of a burial at sea in a burning ship; they got more than his brother. He shivered and sobbed as he watched, and in moments was asleep.

The children were wide eyed and in awe.

"But did Arndt live?" demanded the little girl.

"Yeah!" Asked the smaller boy, "He got bit by the Draug, right?"

"Indeed he did," said the old man.

"What happened after that?" They all said in unison.

"Did he change into a Draug and go home and kill his whole village?" asked the older boy.

"No, he did not. In fact he lived happily ever after. Well…after many years of raiding, great battles in the shield wall, and acquiring magnificent treasure, that is." The old man replied.

"But if he got bitten, how come he didn't change like the others?" asked the young boy.

"Well, it seems that the power in Draug's Bane not only helped kill the monsters, but also protected the wielder from their evil spell."

The children were wide eyed. "Does Arndt still live?" asked the little girl.

"Some say he does…"

"Grandfather, it's time for bed," a young woman said, as she approached the fire. "You little rascals, off to bed yourselves! Shoo!" The children scampered off, delighted with the tale.

"Were you telling ghost stories again, Grandfather?" she asked smiling at him; she draped a blanket around his shoulders.

"What else has an old man to do, dear?"

"How is your shoulder? I know it often aches on cold damp nights like this." She rubbed the old man's shoulders and pulled back his tunic a little to reveal his old scars - A set of large teeth marks! "That damn wound has never healed right has it? Bloody Celtic savages! Biting my grandfather."

The old man smiled and walked back to his cottage with the young woman, Draug's Bane strapped securely to his belt.

THE END

Award Winning Author of The Yggdrasil Codex

I'll Buy you The Moon

A Short Story by: **Hugh B. Long**

I ll Buy You The Moon

(5284 words)

A selfless girl sacrifices everything, struggling to survive in a gritty dystopian future in order to fulfill her little sister's one dream - to see the Moon.

Most people would agree that there are limits to what you can own; owning other people is forbidden, at least in the modern world. But what about everything else? We can own the land, the minerals underground, as well as the sea (within a set number of miles of sovereign territory). But what about the sky? Or even the moon?

In a dystopian future, Mega Corp has covered the globe in a shell, blocking the entire view of the sky. In this world, two sisters share a simple dream - to see the moon in the night sky.

Warning - make sure you have a box of Kleenex or tissues while reading this story!

Exhausted, Hanna stumbled and tripped, slicing open her knee on the crumbling concrete sidewalk. She sat and examined her bloody knee, wincing when she saw the gash. After a sixteen hour shift at the local food processing corporation she could barely keep her eyes open, let alone walk a straight line. Was this a dream? A nightmare? She could scarcely tell. She wanted to wake up, to flee this...whatever it was. Hanna recalled a jagged fragment of a memory, a vignette of the perfect house. It was a single story bungalow with white wood siding, red trim around the windows and doors and a mailbox fashioned like a small red barn. She could even smell fresh bread baking, carried by a sweet and gentle breeze. Was that real?

She got her answer. The illusion was dispelled when a rough hand grabbed her shoulder. She looked up to see a disheveled old man in filthy clothes, minus a few teeth. His hand was gnarled like an old grey oak, knotted, crooked and dirty.

"Darlin, are you ok?" he asked sincerely. There was kindness in his voice, though that kindness was carried on warm, sour breath that nearly made Hanna gag. She breathed through her mouth to avoid further assault.

Hanna nodded, eyes closed, her arms clutched around her knees.

"You sure? That knee don't look too good."

"I'm fine, thank you though," she managed meekly.

"Ok, if you're sure. I'd feel mighty bad if somethin happened to ya." He walked off, mumbling to himself.

Hanna pulled her head to her knees and wept. Her frail body was wracked with tears and the realization that this wasn't a dream, this was real.

She cried until most of the tension was swept from her body. I guess that's what crying's for, she thought. Had to be good for something, most people she knew did lots of it.

Steadying herself on a rusted iron hand rail, she stood, brushed the dirt off her slacks and long black canvas raincoat, and then resumed the hour-long walk home.

It was dark. It was always dark. Mega Corp's shell around the planet gathered solar power, but at the same time prevented unlawful use of the sky (people looking at it). It was their property after all, and without a ticket or a subscription, people had no right to use it.

The shell was composed of hundred-meter-long rectangular sections of a composite material, on top of which was a solar collector; the bottom was a display matrix that delivered advertisements and other messages.

The shell blocked the majority of sunlight, yet allowed enough through to take care of basic human needs. In the agricultural areas the panels were less opaque.

Sixteen hours a day, six days a week, Hanna Strauss worked in a dimly lit factory without a single window - they were redundant these days anyway. It was a steady job though, and the pay was ok; she could afford a small apartment for her and her little sister. They could even buy what passed for food.

Their parents both died of common diseases that were entirely curable, but if you couldn't afford health insurance, you got no treatment; laissez-faire capitalism in action. Her father's death was from colon cancer, which was detected in plenty of time for him to receive treatment from which he would have had a 90% chance of recovering. Her mother got pneumonia, but they couldn't afford the antibiotics and other drugs required to save her. They tried every home remedy they could dig up, but she died three weeks into it. They died a year apart, her father first, and her mother last year. Now Hanna took care of her seven year old sister Clara.

The walk had buoyed Hanna's spirit somewhat; she didn't like coming home to Clara like that - she had to be strong.

Hanna opened the glass door to her apartment building and walked into the lobby. A scrappy looking orange cat with mangled ears, matted fur, and a bold personality, greeted Hanna with a loud "Mreow!"

"Hi, Leo." She smiled, bending over, rubbing the cat behind his ears as he arched his back, pressing against her legs. "My you're a happy fellow!" she laughed. Clara wanted a cat, but they couldn't afford to keep one of their own, so Leo became their part-time adopted pet. He lived somewhere in the building and they gave him little treats whenever they could, but he too had to pull his weight; there wasn't a mouse in a three block radius.

She knocked on the door of apartment #1 which belonged to their landlady, Mrs. Harris. She took care of Clara for a few hours after school while Hanna was working. Clara had been at home sick for a few days so Mrs. Harris was taking care of her full-time - she didn't seem to mind. She was a kind woman, retired, with no children of her own and home all day.

The door opened with a creak. Mrs. Harris stood in the doorway. "Hello, dear, come in. Clara's sleeping."

Hanna stepped into the old apartment, which was filled with forty years of Knicks-knacks - it was a veritable museum. "How was she today?" Hanna asked, with a concerned look.

Mrs. Harris frowned. "Not well, dear. She coughed a lot and brought up some blood. She ate though, and kept everything down. Have you heard back from the doctors?"

"Not yet, but I'm going in tomorrow, hopefully they'll have some good news for us."

A little wisp of a girl with curly blonde hair came into the foyer, rubbing her eyes sleepily. "Hanna?"

"Hi sweet-pea!" Hanna lit up. Since their parents died, Clara was her whole world. "How are you feeling?" She swept Clara up in a tight hug, burying her face in her golden locks.

"Ok," replied Clara.

"Let's go home and get you to bed, alright?" Hanna choked back a tear. She felt so utterly helpless. Here was this little doll, a tiny person who needed her help - and she was failing in that duty. Hanna promised her mother on her deathbed that she would take care of Clara.

Clara nodded, then put her head back down on Hanna's shoulder.

"Thanks again, Mrs. Harris."

The old woman gently put a hand on Hanna's shoulder with a understanding smile. "Anytime, dear. See you tomorrow, Clara."

Hanna carried her little sister up the three flights of stairs to their apartment. She didn't weigh much - she'd lost ten pounds in the last few months. Hanna prayed every night for some end to this illness, surely there was a just God or gods up there listening?

She started thinking about the appointment with the doctor tomorrow - she was hopeful, and terrified at the same time. What if there was something seriously wrong with Clara, she wondered. She knew there must be, she just prayed they could get to the bottom of it and make her well again. She would find a way to pay for whatever Clara needed.

Hanna carried Clara into their spartan apartment - they had long since sold every thing of value - and placed her straight into bed, then tucked her in. Hanna was still wearing her black canvas raincoat and reached into her left pocket, pulling out a faded yellowing picture with worn edges.

"I bought you something today, sweet-pea!"

Clara's sleepy eyes widened. "You did? What did you get me?"

Hanna held the picture in front of Clara's face. It was a postcard-sized picture of the moon.

"Wow! It's beautiful!" Clara took the picture and held it even closer to her eyes, scrutinizing every detail. "I want to see the real thing someday."

Neither she nor Hanna had ever seen the moon. They were both born long after Mega Corp erected the global solar shell, which effectively obscured the view of the entire sky, including the moon. Neither had even seen the sky.

"We'll see it soon, I promise." She kissed Clara on the forehead. "Get some sleep, sweet-pea. I have to see the doctor in the morning, then I have to work the afternoon shift to make up for being gone, so you'll spend the night at Mrs. Harris's tomorrow, ok?"

"Ok."

Clara tucked her new treasure under her pillow, rolled over and closed her eyes.

The following day Hanna began the two hour trek to the clinic where Clara's doctors worked. She watched as a battered city bus rumbled passed her, accelerating with a low pitched whine. It belched thick black diesel fumes which clung to her clothing. Taking the bus to the clinic would have been nice, but Hanna was saving every penny to buy tickets to the lunar observatory; she'd been saving for a couple of years. Two tickets were the equivalent of six months of her wages at the factory, so even with clever scrimping and saving, it would still be another seven months or so before she could buy them; it was Clara's dream though. Their parents had regaled them both with stories of the luminescent giant, tales of wondrous silver light, patterns, and even a face - The Man In The Moon, they said.

That sliver of light at the end of a miserable tunnel kept her going - not the light of moon, but just the light in Clara's eyes when she saw it, that would be Hanna's reward. Sure Hanna wanted to see it, but making her little sister happy was her only wish. That hope sustained her in these dark days. If not for Clara…well…

As she got closer to the more affluent neighborhoods, where all the doctors and hospitals were located, there was an almost hideous contrast - one might think their separation was planned to make them so inconvenient for the poor to get to, that most wouldn't bother. Nobody would be that callous though, Hanna thought.

Where the industrial district and its environs were dark, the burbs were rather more bright, approaching, but not quite cheerful. Several houses had flower beds in their front yards as well as ultra-violet (UV) lights to keep them growing. There was enough sunlight trickling through the shell for basic human needs, but no more. Most flowers required much more sunlight than was common, and so the more affluent had UV lights in their gardens. She stopped in front of one relatively prolific flower garden and smelled a small under-sized red rose - it's fragrance washed the diesel fumes and other urban scents from her nose, at least for the moment she bent over to enjoy it - the floral after scent faded quickly as she stood up and walked again.

Hannah heard a grinding, rolling sound, and looked up. Several blocks away one of the panels in the shell was being pivoted to allow the residents below a view of the sky. They probably had a subscription. Lucky, she thought. For a rather steep fee, residents could subscribe to the sky, and depending on the rates they paid, they would get an unobstructed view for a period commensurate with the fee. On nights when there were exceptional celestial events, such as a full moon, a transit of Venus, or the Northern Lights, the fees for viewing were, well, astronomical. The really wealthy had the panels above their homes permanently pivoted open.

As she walked, one of the panels above flashed an advertisement.

"MEGA CORP ORGAN BANK"

Sell your organs for cash!
Kidneys, eyes, lungs, testicles.
You have 2, why not sell one?
Short on cash? Behind on the rent?
Want a special holiday?
We can help!"

She shook her head and kept walking. She knew people figuratively sold their bodies - there were many street walkers living around her building, but to literally sell a piece of yourself? How low would you have to be to do that, she wondered. Then she looked around and soaked in the scenery, banishing those dark thoughts, for a little while anyway.

There was a coffee shop on the street that Hanna was walking on, and it occurred to her that she hadn't had anything to drink in hours, and she was very thirsty. Maybe she would stop and get a drink of water. She couldn't afford a coffee or anything else, but water would do. Maybe it was even better than the water in her building, she thought. Their water was frequently colored with brown gunk, and tasted…well, there were no words to describe it really.

Hanna walked into the coffee-shop, the door chiming as she entered. The several patrons in there, glanced at her, and then looked away. She walked up to the counter and stood by the cash register; there was nobody else in line.

An older portly man with slicked back hair and a name-tag that read 'Brett' sauntered over to the section of the counter where Hanna was standing.

"Good morning, miss. What can I get for you?" he asked.

"May I have a cup of water please?"

Brett eyed her up and down, a near scowl forming on his face. He leaned down towards her. "I can't give away cups. That's how my boss counts his money, by the cup. Did you want to buy something?"

"Um, no. I just wanted water," Hanna shook her head, feeling very embarrassed. She could feel her cheeks flushing.

Maybe she could get some water form the bathroom tap?

"Is there a bathroom I can use?" She asked.

"I'm sorry, miss, the bathroom is for paying customers only," he said.

Hanna had no reply. She was near the breaking point at all times, barely able to keep herself together. "Ok," she choked out, a tear welling in her eye. She walked out of the coffee-shop, back out to the street. She looked into the window of the coffee shop as some older woman stepped up to the counter. Brett produced what looked like a glass of water, all smiles.

Hanna looked at her reflection in the shop window: She saw a girl with a dirty face, disheveled hair and thread bare clothes. She looked like a proper street urchin, not the steadfast, reliable factory worker that she was. In that reflection she saw a glimmer of what those people must see: a shadow of a human being, a person that was, or that could be, but wasn't; but desperately wanted to be.

The clinic was soon in view. It was beautiful: the building had clean lines, a rich stone facade near the ground and spotless glass windows. How did they keep those windows clean, she wondered? She walked into a lobby where an archetypical overweight security guard sat on a chair behind a small desk. Information was stenciled on the desk. She knew where she was going, so no need to bother the guard, but he had other ideas.

"Excuse me, miss?" He said, standing up.

Hanna turned back to him.

"Can I help you?"

"No, thank you," Hanna replied

The guard stepped out from behind the desk. "Where are you headed, miss? He asked.

"I'm headed to Doctor Kehr's office on the twelfth floor"

That seemed to placate him. "Ok, just trying to make sure you didn't need any help, miss."

Hanna forced a half smile and turned back to the elevator. She pressed the UP button, and waited for the car to come retrieve her. With the requisite - DING - the doors whisked open, Hanna stepped in and was on her way to the twelfth floor.

The car was empty but she was accompanied by ridiculously cheerful music. How many people appreciated this garbage, she wondered. People were most likely here to see about some dire medical issue and they play this silly music?

Nobody thought seriously about anything beyond their narrow purview. Somebody in some corporate office decided that sick people might need cheering up. Why don't we give them some pleasant music for their elevator trip? Great idea - Assholes! Hanna berated herself for her caustic thoughts. They were just trying to get by like everyone else she decided. But it was still terrible music.

Hanna checked in with the receptionist; she was glamorous looking twenty-something with blonde hair and finger nails that could barely manage a keyboard. Hanna wished she had hair like that though; it was a silky yellow mane that hung down to the middle of her back. Then Hanna noticed the barest trace of a transition - her hairs were implants or extensions. Not real at all. A facade like so much else.

She took a seat and began rummaging through old magazines. Better Homes & Gardens? Who lives like that?' Hanna mused. She leafed through pages of dream homes and dream lives, wishing she could transport herself into the pages of that idyllic world.

"Miss Strauss?" the receptionist called and stood to usher her in.

"Yes." Hanna stood and followed her to the doctors office.

The receptionist gestured to an open door. In the office was a balding man in his fifties, wearing a cream colored shirt and tie with a white overcoat.

"Good morning, Miss Strauss, please, take a seat," said Dr. Kehr.

Hanna sat in a lightly padded chair in front of the doctor's desk. "Are all the results back from Clara's tests?" she asked.

"Yes, they are," he replied, then paused.

"Well? What's wrong with my sister?"

"I wish I had better news, Hanna. Clara is suffering from late stage cystic fibrosis."

Hanna felt like she had been run over by a car. Her whole body was numb; she was dazed. Cystic fibrosis?

"What's the cure? What do we do next?" she said, almost panicky.

"There is no cure, Hanna. It's chronic…and often fatal."

Hanna's eyes were burning; she could feel tears running down her cheeks. It couldn't be real. He must be wrong, she thought.

"In Clara's case," he continued, "it's very advanced. Many people with CF live into their thirties, but in Clara's case we might have weeks."

"What?" Hanna screamed the words. "You can't be serious?" Hanna stood. "Weeks? How?"

"This is a very rare case, Hanna, I'm sorry. We can help make her comfortable though, that's the best we can hope for."

Hanna was still standing, shaking her head. She walked out of the doctor's office, and entered the elevator in a silent daze. As the elevator door opened, she broke into a run and darted out of the building. She ran for a while, she didn't remember how long, then just slowed down to a walking pace.

Hanna shambled along under the dim streets until her feet felt like they would break if she took another step. Every time she imagined seeing Clara again, she started sobbing. She tried desperately to get control of herself; she didn't want to upset Clara by arriving home in this state. Her poor little sweet pea. All she wanted was to see the moon. And now she would never get that chance. Hanna was still many months away from saving the money necessary to buy their tickets - it would be too late for Clara by the time she had it all.

At 4:35am the next morning, five minutes late for her shift, Hanna arrived at the food processing factory where she worked. It was a large two story building that stretched on for a kilometer, seemingly anyway. The exterior was shabby and a constant thrum of industry escaped from inside. There were machines and people and forklifts all moving and grinding and working.

She worked in the frozen food packaging section. It was by necessity, damn cold in there - freezing in fact. The smells of the raw meat and blood of various species were muted by the cold and this effect added to the overall strangeness of it.

Although she wore gloves, Hanna's hands were numb after an hour of stuffing frozen chicken parts into boxes, yet she pressed on, shaking her hands occasionally to try to restore some feeling.

"Hanna," a co-worker shouted.

She looked over to see Carl, a friendly middle-aged man; he ate lunch with Hanna some days. Hanna pulled one of her ear-muffs off to hear him. "What is it, Carl?" she shouted.

"Mr. Florence wants to see you in his office." He said.

Hanna let her ear-muff snap back on and nodded her head. This would not be good. Florence was the shop foreman.

She exited the noisy environment of the shop floor and entered the only slightly less noisy section of offices and cubicles. Mr. Florence's office had no windows and a thick steel door. She knocked.

"C'mon in," a voice said.

Hanna entered to find Mr. Florence sitting behind his desk, adorned by a handsomely framed picture of him with his wife, son and daughter - she looked to be about Hanna's age. He wasn't an ugly man, not handsome though, maybe in his forties and definitely out of shape. He wore a gold crucifix around his neck, displayed prominently, declaring himself to be a Christian. He beckoned to her with his hand. "Close the door behind you."

Hanna entered, her head down slightly.

"Have a seat, Hanna," he said with a broad smile, pointing to a chair in front of his desk. Hanna sat.

"Do you know why I asked you here today, Hanna?"

Hanna shook her head. Although she figured she did know - she was five minutes late this morning.

"I'm concerned about you, Hanna." Florence got up from his desk and walked behind Hanna.

Hanna was looking at plaques hanging on his wall. One was Recognition from Johnsville Baptist Church for his service as a Summer Camp Minister for Teens last summer.

"You've been late a lot lately, Hanna. That concerns me. As one of my team, I want to make sure everything here is going well for you.

Hanna heard a click. Was that the door locking?

"We're like a family here, Hanna," he continued, "when something is wrong, we help each other. That's what families do, right?"

Hanna nodded, and swallowed. He was standing behind her now, and she could smell cigarette on his breath.

"Can you tell me what's been going on?" he asked.

"My sister, sir - "

"Call me Doug," he interrupted.

"Doug...my sister has been pretty sick. I'm sorry I've been late. I'll make it up or you can dock my pay or something. It won't happen again," she said nervously.

She felt his hand on her right shoulder.

"It's ok, Hanna. Like I said, we're like family. We take care of each other. I take care of you, you take care of me." His hand slid off her shoulder, down the front of her chest and cupped her breast.

She stopped breathing all together, frozen with panic.

"I imagine that if your sister is sick then you need this job right?" he continued.

Hanna forced a small nod. She felt her stomach churning.

"See, well that's good. I'll help you keep this job. I'll look past this tardiness. I'm an understanding guy." He had both hands on her chest now, pressing his groin against the back of her neck.

Hanna squeezed here eyes tight.

"Now, since I'm helping you, I want you to do something for me, ok?" Hanna forced another nod. She needed this job; they were barely hanging on as is. If she lost this job they might be on the streets, Clara couldn't survive that.

There was a loud knock on Florence's door.

"Doug, do you have a minute?" came a man's voice form the other side.

"I'm in a meeting!" he shouted. "Come back in a half hour."

He was stroking Hanna's hair now, she began to tremble slightly and felt woozy. He pulled her chair around forcefully so she was facing him. He had a wide, hungry smile on his face. He unbuttoned his pants and they slid to the floor and stopped around his ankles.

"You'll do something for me now, right?" he was breathing very heavy now.

Hanna opened her eyes and vomited all over Florence. It kept coming almost ballistically and she vomited again.

Florence fell back, tripping on his own pants that were around his ankles. He was covered in steaming yellowish vomit from his chest to his feet.

"You little bitch!"

Hanna stood up, confused, saying nothing.

"Just get the fuck out of here!" he said, trying to pick himself up.

Hanna fumbled with the lock on the door and burst out of the room.

Several people in the hall looked at Hanna running, and a couple peeked into Florence's office to find him with his pants down, standing in a pool of vomit.

A week after Hanna consulted with the doctors and her incident with Doug Florence, Clara seemed to be deteriorating at an ever more rapid pace. Clara's breathing was more and more labored; she could no longer go to school and could barely get out of bed.

Mrs. Harris was minding Clara full time now and kindly offered to let the girls move in with her; she had plenty of room, and it would make it easier for her to take care of Clara, and save Hanna some money, which the girls needed.

Hanna arrived home from work and sat down on the couch. She fell asleep almost instantly. Mrs. Harris shook her shoulder lightly.

"Hanna? Long day, dear? I can warm up some dinner if you're hungry."

"Huh? Oh, no, I'm not hungry, thanks. I've got a present for Clara, I'll go in and give it to her."

"She's already sound asleep, dear. Why don't you give it to her in the morning."

"Ok, good idea." Hanna lay down, adjusting a cushion on the couch and rolled over, facing the back of the couch.

Mrs. Harris looked back at Hannah, happy to see her comfortable, but noticed a dark stain on the lower back of Hanna's shirt - it looked wet. She walked over and inspected the stain on the shirt; it was dark and sticky. Blood, she wondered? She shook Hanna's shoulder. "Hanna?"

"Hmm?" Hanna groaned, half asleep.

"Dear, there's a stain on the back of your shirt; it looks like blood," she said.

"It's ok, Mrs. Harris, I got cut at work. It's nothing serious."

Mrs. Harris frowned, clearly unconvinced. She shook her head and pulled an old beige crocheted blanket over Hanna, who was already fast asleep.

The next morning the girls awoke to the smell of bacon and eggs. Clara hadn't much of an appetite lately, but she loved bacon - extra crispy was her favorite.

Hanna carried Clara to the table and helped her take a seat. Hanna winced as she stood up.

"You ok, Hanna?" Clara asked.

"I'm fine sweet pea, just a cramp in my back. I had a long day yesterday." Hanna said.

Clara smiled up at her.

Mrs. Harris walked over to the kitchen table with a cast iron skillet which held the prized crispy bacon, along with scrambled eggs.

"Who wanted bacon?" Mrs. Harris asked.

Clara threw up her hand with a muted squeal. "Me!"

"Oh, are you sure? I didn't think you liked bacon, Clara." Mrs. Harris teased.

"I love bacon." Clara said, as if to clarify this point once and for all. Clara's jubilation over breakfast started a coughing fit which lasted a few minutes and drained her of her previous energy.

After Clara recovered, Mrs. Harris served the girls hearty portions, and then sat down herself to eat. The three enjoyed each other's company and a full breakfast table.

When they were done eating, Hanna spoke. "Clara, I have something for you - for us." Hanna placed a crumpled, re-used envelope, on the table. Clara forced a weak smile and opened the envelope. She pulled out two silver tickets with scalloped gold edges. Each read:

[Admit One - Lunar Park - Valid 7:00pm to 11:00pm]

"Thank you, Ha- " Clara began coughing violently, and dropped the tickets. Hanna and Mrs. Harris helped Clara to the bathroom where she coughed up a large pool of blackish-red blood. Her coughing finally subsided after a few minutes.

Clara looked at Hanna. "Are we going after you get home from work?"

"I'm not going to work today, sweet-pea, I need some rest before we go." She smiled at Hanna, grey bags below her eyes, underscoring her fatigue.

Mrs. Harris was thoughtful enough to borrow a stroller from a woman in another apartment. She knew Clara wouldn't make the walk to the park, and sadly, with all the weight Clara recently lost, she would fit in the stroller with room to spare.

With Clara sitting safely, Hanna pushed the stroller slowly along - she was exhausted. Neither girl spoke much on the trip to the Lunar Park; they were both on autopilot of sorts.

An illuminated sign with silvery-white lettering lit up the area in front of Lunar Park. Hanna could see the panels above the park opened to the sky. Even at this angle she could see the sky, just a little, several stars peaking out at them from the twilight sky.

"Look, Clara! The stars."

Clara opened her eyes, a small smile appearing on her weary face.

"They're pretty," said Clara, "Where's the moon?"

"It'll be out soon, sweet-pea. We'll go find a place to sit and wait for it arrive."

"Do they have to call it?"

Hanna laughed. "No, sweet-pea, it's always moving, we just have to wait till it gets here. It'll only be a few more minutes." Clara began coughing, and gasping for air. "Just try to relax...keep calm, breath slow."

Clara nodded.

Hanna pushed the stroller through the park until she found an open level stretch of grass - a spot where she might have had a picnic in the old days. She brought the old crocheted blanket from Mrs. Harris's and spread on the ground; she leaned against the stroller listening to Clara's breathing slow. She closed her eyes. She thought of her parents and wished they were here to share this moment with them, but she knew she'd see them soon.

"Hanna! Look! The Moon! It's so beautiful." Clara's eyes were beaming. She marveled at the pale, silvery-warm glow. She looked carefully for the face her parents used to tell them about. "There's the man in the moon, Hanna! I see it!" She coughed once, but quickly got it under control. Neither spoke as the moon painted a gentle arc across the sky, transiting the span of the ten open panels. Shortly, only the stars remained to decorate the dark firmament.

"Thank you, Hanna. That was the best present ever. I'll never forget this." Hanna didn't respond, she lay quietly, yes closed.

"Hanna? Are you ok?"

Beside Hanna, on the ground near her coat pocket, was a white piece of paper - a receipt:

```
----- MEGA CORP ORGAN BANK -----
----- Receipt for 2 Kidneys -----
----- Payment: Direct Deposit -----
```

THE END

A Short Story by: Hugh B. Long

Crime & Punishment

(2183 words)

For thousands of years society has imposed various punishments for what they define as crime. Laws and their enforcement are the foundations of a stable civilization.

So what constitutes a crime? And for the most heinous crimes, what's an appropriate punishment?

In the short story, Crime & Punishment, the lives of two individuals collide: The first, a devious criminal called Vargr, and the second, an ordinary man named Charles Wilson.

Vargr knew he shouldn't have done it, but in a moment of weakness he did, and now he was in a stark prison cell. His mind was panicking at the thought of his sentence. There was only one punishment for any crime among his people; the punishment was harsh, very harsh.

His cell was dark and cold, presaging his life to come. The gloom suffused his soul. He desperately grasped at some glimmer of hope - his family - but what would they think? There were no visitors where he was going. Prison meant seclusion and a revocation of all rights and privileges accorded to normal citizens. Vargr tried to steel himself. There was no point in despairing, he committed a crime and he was being punished. Cause and effect. If only his rationale mind had asserted itself before he did the deed.

He was jolted from his musings by a loud beeping over the intercom in his cell. "Prisoner Vargr, please move back while I open the cell door. It's time for sentencing."

His insides felt like a writhing nest of snakes.

Vargr moved back while the cell door was opened. The stern look of the guard melted Vargr into compliance - not that he was going to resist. He was lead to a dark chamber, he saw no light whatsoever, but judging by echoes of various sounds, it must be cavernous. The guard stopped.

"Remain at this spot. Do not attempt to move until instructed to do so." The guard retreated into the darkness behind Vargr.

Vargr remained still, feeling like a bundle of raw nerves. He'd never experienced a sentencing nor learned of what went on at one. Criminals who served their time and were introduced back into society were forbidden to share anything related to it, on pain of execution of themselves and their family.

A light shot down from the ceiling and illuminated a wizened citizen - the magistrate presumably.

"Citizen Vargr, or should I say Prisoner Vargr, you are here before me today convicted of a heinous crime. Do you have anything to communicate prior to learning your sentence?"

"I do not." he replied. What could he say? He was guilty, he was sorry, but none of it mattered now.

"Very well, by the authority of my office, I sentence you to a lifetime in prison. The sentence shall commence immediately."

The guard returned and lead Vargr out of the chamber.

"Beep - Beep - Beep - Beep," blared Charles Wilson's alarm. He leaned over and saw glowing red LEDs indicating the time - 6:00am. It was Monday morning, time to get up and go to work. Charles rolled out of bed with a big yawn, stretching his arms, standing slowly.

Charles trundled over to his ensuite bathroom for his morning pee. 'Pretty clear,' he thought. 'Good, I guess I'm hydrating properly.' He stepped over to the sink and picked up his blue toothbrush, applied some red cinnamon odored paste, and began his ritual brushing. Fifty brush strokes on each side, upper and lower jaw. That accomplished, he fumbled for his floss in the top left drawer of the sink. He wrapped the floss around his hand exactly four times, then cut it - enough to wrap around each hand and floss each tooth comfortably. Once done, he rinsed his mouth, and made his way into the shower. He squirted out a quarter sized gob of shampoo, applied it to his hair and massaged it in twenty times, then rinsed. Picking up a bar of soap, he applied three foamy strokes on each body part, then stood under the stream of water and rinsed his entire body. He stepped over the short glass lip of the shower and picked up his towel, rubbed his hair four times then moved on to drying the rest of his body.

Once his morning bathroom routine concluded, Charles went to his bedroom wardrobe to select his day's clothes. Sliding the wardrobe open produced a low rumbling sound. On the top racks were a dozen white collared shirts, and below them, a dozen pairs of charcoal pants. He looked over the selection and picked the first shirt and pair of pants from the leftmost side of his closet. Once dressed, Charles headed into the kitchen where he poured one cup of cereal into a bowl, onto which went a half cup of skimmed milk. 'A very healthy breakfast,' he thought. Charles avoided any caffeinated beverages; they gave him insomnia.

As he did every morning when he left the house for work, he picked up the daily newspaper from his porch, scanning the headlines as he made his way to the bus stop. A white city bus stopped, he entered, and was whisked off to his destination at a municipal pace.

Standing testimony to progress and industry was the twenty story grey stone office building where Charles worked Monday through Friday, 9:00am to 5:00am, for fifty weeks a year. He did get two weeks of vacation which was usually spent at a modest motel on the seashore. He enjoyed that quiet time to read a book, or work on his tan. But today was a workday.

Upon entering the lobby of the office building, Charles sauntered up to the elevator and walked in to an already open car which a young red head was holding open for him. He pressed the button for the third floor, then stood quietly, looking up, or at the floor. Careful not to make eye contact. After all he didn't want to bother anyone, and he hated small talk - what a waste of time. A DING sounded and the light on the third floor button was illuminated, the elevator door slid open with that ever unnerving clunking sound.

Charles stepped out and after a twenty foot walk and two right turns, he approached a sea of cubicles, all separated by chest-high walls of dull grey fabric. He nodded perfunctorily to various co-workers who had arrived before him and proceeded fifteen cubes down and five over, arriving at his personal workspace. His L-shaped work area was devoid of any clutter, save for a picture of his mother. He dearly loved the old bird. Charles put his newspaper down and turned on his computer. While it booted-up, he made his way over to the break room.

As he arrived he smelled the odour of burnt coffee; a pot left empty on a hot element. 'Damnit,' he thought. The person who took the last cup hadn't been considerate enough to brew the next pot. 'Some people...no respect at all.' Charles picked up a pre-packaged packet of coffee in a self-contained filter and placed it in the brewing basket, he next filled the pot with cold water then carefully poured it into the back of the machine; he pressed the START button, and with a THUD the machine began brewing a fresh pot of coffee. It took about fifteen minutes to brew so Charles figured he'd go back to his cube and check his e-mail - he liked to maximize use of his time; .he was a responsible employee and took great pride in that.

After a few emails had been read, or deleted in the case of SPAM, he made his way back to the break room. He picked up a mug and as he reached for the coffee pot to fill it, he noticed it was empty - Again! 'God damnit!' he fumed internally. 'Thoughtless bastards, and they couldn't be bothered to start a new pot!' He could feel his face going red. He went back to his cube, picked up a yellow sticky note, scribbled something hastily, then made his way back to the break room; he stuck the note on the side of the machine and stomped off. The note read: "If you finish a pot, please put on a fresh one. Thank you." That's not what he wanted to write, but it was the polite response.

His office work was satisfying; he enjoyed carefully analyzing all the bills that came to the company. His official title was 'Assistant Manager - Accounts Payable'. He'd gotten the promotion recently. It didn't come with a pay raise, but he was pleased with the title and all the new responsibilities. Charles Wilson had a good life. He was fifty-two years old, had a modest house, a respectable job, and his health (if you didn't count his bum knee which ached in sync with stormy weather). Although he'd never married, he'd dated a few nice girls, and today he had lunch with Elaine Carson; she was a middle aged divorcee who worked across the street. He was looking forward to it.

12:00pm and his impending lunch date came quickly. Charles made a stop to use the bathroom before heading down to meet Elaine. He looked in the mirror, straightened his greying black hair, then pulled a small aerosol tube breath freshener out of his pocket. Three squirts later he was out the bathroom door and on his way to the elevator.

A couple of others were also waiting to go down, so no need to press the button. He stood quietly until he heard the elevator doors open, then waited politely for the others to board first, even though he was closer. Upon reaching the ground floor he noticed how sunny it was, and felt in his pocket for a pair of foldable sunglasses - always a practical accessory. He put them on and stepped out onto the sidewalk, heading right towards the intersection and the crosswalk to Elaine's building. A red hand was illuminated so he stood obediently waiting for it to change color, and it did in short order - the green hand signalling his turn to cross.

As he walked across the intersection, he saw Elaine. 'Wow, she looks great today," he thought. His last thought in fact - ever. He didn't see the truck run the red light while he focused on Elaine, nor did the driver, rushing through the yellow light, notice the nondescript man crossing the street.

With a sickening THUMP and SPLAT the dingy yellow dump truck obliterated Charles Wilson, killing him instantly; his body, a red pulpy mass, was dragged beneath the dump truck as it screeched to a halt.

Vargr shuddered, feeling confused and very disoriented. 'Where am I?' he wondered, 'is this prison?' He remembered an oppressive darkness, a constriction, the feeling of being bound. Terrifying.

His consciousness began to clear, like a stiff breeze dispelling a morning fog. A guard was next to him, and in front of him was the wizened Magistrate. Yes, he remembered now. He was sentenced to a lifetime in prison for his crime. Why was he so dazed?

The Magistrate was looking down on the floor at an elliptical, misty-edged projection - on which was a strange scene with corporeal beings walking around in great numbers, some running frantically and a large yellow object striking one of them. "Oh my stars!" Vargr exclaimed. "I remember! I remember everything!" He began trembling, vibrating, his orange energetic mass undulating in response to this disturbance in his energy matrix.

The Magistrate's blueish spherical form glowed in a flashing pattern as he laughed. "Do you like what you remember, Vargr?"

"No! It was horrible! By all that's negatively charged, how could you do that to me? I was immutable, I had one form, and so limited! I never realized that such terror was possible. And the daily routine! What diabolical mind conceived of such torments?"

"Yes, Vargr, it was terrible. That was our intention. Our society has never had a repeat offender since we built the Terran prison planet. For two million years our system of justice has kept the peace. When a citizen is convicted of a crime, he is imprisoned in a human, his cell, on the Terran prison planet; there to live out the most unspeakably limited existence. With one form, unable to freely roam the galaxies. Everything about it is anathema to our kind, and even that short incarceration - the length of one of their brief human lifetimes - has always been enough to ensure a 0% recidivism. You were extremely fortunate. Your cell, Charles Wilson, died accidentally at age fifty-two. You might have endured another forty years of your sentence and agonized over the slow and painful decay of his body. You should give thanks to the stellar nursery that chance granted you an early parole."

Vargr had no words. He understood now why there were no repeat offenders. No energetic being would ever choose that horribly limited, constrictive corporeal existence.

"You're free to go Vargr. You understand the ramifications if you ever speak of any of this?"

"Yes, Magistrate."

"Very well, free citizen Vargr, be on your way."

Vargr floated out of the magnetically sealed room and made for home.

"Next prisoner!" barked the Magistrate.

THE END